Delores B a Fortune

Pam Rapoza

AuthorHouse™
1663 Liberty Drive
Bloomington, IN 47403
www.authorhouse.com
Phone: 1 (800) 839-8640

Published by AuthorHouse 08/31/2018

ISBN: 978-1-5462-5468-3 (sc)
ISBN: 978-1-5462-5469-0 (e)

Library of Congress Control Number: 2018909585

Print information available on the last page.

Any people depicted in stock imagery provided by Getty Images are models, and such images are being used for illustrative purposes only. Certain stock imagery © Getty Images.

This book is printed on acid-free paper.

Because of the dynamic nature of the Internet, any web addresses or links contained in this book may have changed since publication and may no longer be valid. The views expressed in this work are solely those of the author and do not necessarily reflect the views of the publisher, and the publisher hereby disclaims any responsibility for them.

authorHOUSE®

Delores Bakes a Fortune

You are an exceptional baker, and you are one smart cookie!

Pam Rapoza

P.S.
Pam was one of my teachers
@ ABCD Geneva

Trust your CRAZY ideas!

♥ Pam Rapoza

Delores was a sensitive bird with a sentimental heart.
There was no bird in all of Woodland Grove as sweet
and caring.

She liked to knit, but wasn't very good at it.

She liked to ice-skate, but wasn't very good at it.

She liked to bake, but wasn't very good at it.

What she DID know was that she was exceptional at being a friend. All of her closest friends knew they could always count on Delores.

When they were sick, she was there to help out.

When it was their birthday, she always told a joke to make them laugh.

When they needed a shoulder to cry on, she would cry with them.

After all, that is what good friends do…and Delores was a good friend. She believed that about herself, and it was true. Making people feel good was Delores' specialty.

Delores loved all her friends, but most of all she loved Merv. Merv was her BEST friend. He understood Delores and her silly ways and he loved her anyway. No matter what happened or what she did wrong, Merv stuck by her. After all, that is what you do when you believe in someone, and Merv believed in Delores.

Every day was a new adventure for Delores. She had crazy ideas, and Merv always told her, "Trust your crazy ideas!" So when Delores heard about the Woodland Grove Baking Competition, she got one of her crazy ideas!

She would enter the competition and become the first bird in her family to win the honor of having her recipe printed in *The Gobbler*, the Woodland Grove newspaper.

She liked to bake, and even though she wasn't a good baker, she wanted to win more than anything in the world. *After all*, Delores thought, *winners are people who want it very badly, right?*

Delores set her mind on winning. She practiced making her honey birdseed treats for all the neighborhood chicks. The redbreast twins next door told her they were the worst they had ever eaten!

"I know," sighed Delores, "but they are made with more love than you will ever get in one cookie!"

"Well, that doesn't make them taste any better!" said the twins.

Determined to win, Delores tried to make chocolate nut bark for Merv to nibble on. Merv chomped the candy while Delores watched. She knew it wasn't very tasty, but she really had tried hard. She thought he might like it. Merv just smiled and said, "This tastes like bark, dear."

"I know," cooed Delores, "but I really want to win this contest! I will figure something else out."

After all, thought Delores, *if you want something bad enough and you work very hard at it you will get it, right?*

Delores knew she was not the best baker in the world, but she kept on trying. She knew that her effort would pay off in the end.

Delores finally found a fortune cookie recipe and mastered it in only three days! She even figured out how to write little messages to place inside the cookies for the person eating one to find. What a fun way to make people happy, by sending them messages that make them feel good! That was Delores' specialty, making people feel good.

Delores spent weeks practicing her fortune cookie recipe. She made some for old Mrs. Gooseberry next door. The messages inside told her that she was a good neighbor, and all her friends appreciated her. Mrs. Gooseberry loved the messages but always threw the cookies away. They didn't taste very good.

On the day of the baking competition, Delores gathered all the baking tools she needed for her famous fortune cookies. She prepared special messages for the judges so that when they opened their cookies, they would find messages to make them feel good. Delores was wonderful at making people feel good, but she was not good at baking. She knew that, but she was prepared to try her very best anyway.

The baking competition
did not go well. Deflated,
she moped all the way home and
found Merv sitting in his favorite over-stuffed chair.
Merv noticed how down she looked, and he knew
right away that she had lost.

Delores sat down next to Merv and cried her very hardest cry. "I don't understand. I tried my very best and worked so hard. How silly of me to think a bird could win a baking contest making Chinese cookies! I know I am not a good baker, but I tried so hard and wanted to win more than anyone!"

Merv wiped a tear from Delores' rosy cheek and looked into her sad and defeated eyes. "My dear, we don't get what we **WANT**, we get what we **BELIEVE**."

Delores looked up at Merv in confusion. "I don't understand. I believe I deserved to win! I worked so hard!"

"Yes," chirped Merv, "but you do not believe that you can bake well. You keep telling yourself that you are not a good baker. An excellent baker needs to win a baking competition. It doesn't matter if you want to win, it only matters that you believe you can."

Delores sat quietly with a contemplative look on her face. Merv was right. All the things Delores believed about herself were true. She believed she was a good friend, and she was. Wanting something and **believing** you can do something are two very different things. Delores suddenly realized that if she was ever going to become a great baker, she had to change the belief that she wasn't very good at it.

"Why do you think it is so important for you to win this baking contest?" asked Merv. "Well, I thought it was to prove that I can bake," cried Delores. "Will someone giving you a prize prove that?" Merv wondered aloud.

Delores could not respond. She knew Merv was right … he always was. She did not need to win a prize to prove she could bake. She knew that she could if she set her mind to it.

Delores made an effort to believe she could bake. Every week she made two dozen fortune cookies with the same fortune inside:

You are an exceptional baker, and you are one smart cookie!

One day, Mrs. Gooseberry came to Delores' kitchen door and knocked politely.

"Delores, my friend Erma is sick. I was wondering if you would help me make her feel better? I tried making some of those friendly fortune cookies you make. While the cookies came out great, the messages were very difficult for me to come up with. I'm not such a great writer, like you. Could you help me write some messages for my cookies?"

Just then, Delores' heart did a little leap, and she had a wonderful idea. Mrs. Gooseberry would teach her how to bake, and she would teach Mrs. Gooseberry how to write! It was a perfect partnership, and both of them would learn something new!

For the next few weeks, Delores worked very hard to learn baking skills from her expert friend, Mrs. Gooseberry, while making cookies for the neighbors with fortunes that made everyone happy.

Every day, Delores opened a new fortune cookie and reminded herself that she actually was good at baking. She became well known in Woodland Grove for her tasty and considerate fortune cookies. Creatures drove for miles to buy them. No one could get enough of Delores' Good Fortune Cookies!

Delores knew that she was a good friend. She also knew she could do whatever she set her mind to do. She learned to become great at baking, and she didn't need to win the Woodland Grove Baking Competition to prove that.

After all, thought Delores, *when you believe in someone, especially yourself, you succeed!*

Delores cleaned up her kitchen for the evening and brought Merv a freshly baked fortune cookie and a glass of warm milk to his favorite chair in the living room. She smiled at him and set the cookie down on the table next to him.

"You and your crazy ideas," smirked Merv. They both chuckled. Delores kissed Merv on his handsome beak and went to bed.

Merv opened the warm fortune cookie and pulled out the famous fortune Delores had created. He smiled as he read it:

You don't get what you WANT, you get what you BELIEVE!

CPSIA information can be obtained
at www.ICGtesting.com
Printed in the USA
BVHW02s1127150918
527587BV00007B/23/P